Special thanks to Ryan Ferguson, Kristine Lombardi, Debra Mostow Zakarin, Stuart Smith, Sammie Suchland, Nicole Corse, Charnita Belcher, Julia Phelps, Julia Pistor, Hillary Powell, Garrett Sander, Kris Fogel, Lauren Rose, Sarah Serata, Renevee Romero, and Snowball Studios

Published in the United States by Golden Books, an imprint of Random House Children's Books, a division of Penguin Random House LLC, 1745 Broadway, New York, NY 10019, and in Canada by Penguin Random House Canada Limited, Toronto. No part of this book may be reproduced or copied in any form without permission from the copyright owner. Golden Books, A Golden Book, A Big Golden Book, the G colophon, and the distinctive gold spine are registered trademarks of Penguin Random House LLC.

randomhousekids.com

ISBN 978-1-5247-0117-8

Printed in the United States of America
10 9 8 7 6 5 4 3 2 1

Barbie™ DREAMTOPIA

Based on the original screenplay by Kate Boutilier

Illustrated by Patrick Ian Moss and Charles Pickens

A GOLDEN BOOK • NEW YORK

It was a beautiful sunny day in Malibu. Barbie was busy getting ready for the annual Fun Days Festival with Teresa, Nikki, and Derek. Barbie couldn't wait for Fun Days. Every year the festival was filled with lots of fun and creative activities. There was a bicycle race, a soap bubble race, a mermaid photo booth, a glitter-rock hunt, and . . . costumes!

Meanwhile, Barbie's sister Chelsea was outside playing make-believe with her puppy, Honey.

Chelsea's friends Jace and Zoie stopped by to tell her they had signed up for the Fun Days bicycle race—and they had signed up Chelsea, too!

Chelsea pretended to be excited, but after her friends left, she made a confession to Honey. "I still can't ride a bike without training wheels," she said.

How could she compete in the Fun Days bike race?

Just then, Chelsea's annoying
neighbor, Otto, interrupted.
   "You're never gonna ride that bike
without training wheels," he said.
"Never!"

Chelsea wished her sisters Stacie and Skipper weren't away at summer camp. If they were home, they could help her with her bike—and Otto!

Maybe Otto was right. Maybe she wouldn't be able to ride her bike without training wheels in the race.

Later that night, Barbie gave Chelsea a memory box to make all her sisters feel close. It contained Skipper's headband, Barbie's pink quartz, Stacie's swimming goggles, and a brand-new candy necklace.

"You can add your own memories this summer to share with Skipper and Stacie when they come home," Barbie said.

Then Barbie told Chelsea a story about a winged unicorn.

Chelsea fell asleep and had a wonderful dream—with Barbie in it! In the dream, Chelsea and Honey rode a boat in a pink-lemonade river. They entered a land where everything was made out of candy!

"You're in Sweetville!" said Barbie. She had bubble wings and was known as the Sugar Spun Fairy. Chelsea was delighted!

Just then, Chelsea was about to go over Lemonade Falls. Barbie waved her lollipop wand and gave Chelsea magical bubble wings. Chelsea clutched Honey as they flew upward! Chelsea couldn't wait to see the rest of Sweetville.

"Cupcake houses! Strawberry chairs!" Chelsea exclaimed after landing in Whipped-Cream Cove. "Everything here is made of something sweet," Barbie explained.

"This place is amazing!" Chelsea said. "It reminds me of a story I heard about a winged unicorn."

"You know about the Winged Unicorn?" asked Barbie. "They say it's wild, but whoever rides it will be filled with magic forever."

Chelsea's eyes lit up. "I want to ride it," she said. Magic was exactly what she needed if she was going to race in the Fun Days bicycle race.

A chocolate bunny appeared. "Sugar Spun Fairy, I have terrible news! Our creations are being destroyed," he said, pointing to his half-eaten chocolate ear.

Barbie asked Chelsea to help her find out who was responsible.

As Chelsea raced off to help her new friends, a boy appeared.
"Run all you want, Chelsea," he murmured to himself. "You'll
never ride that Winged Unicorn. Never!"

Barbie and Chelsea soon discovered that the Strawberry Bears were causing the destruction—but only because they were hungry.

"We get extra hungry after we hibernate," one bear explained sheepishly.

Chelsea and Barbie had an idea. The sweet folk could create food just for the hungry bears!

The plan worked! The bears were no longer hungry, and the villagers could live in peace.

Suddenly, the boy appeared again.

"My name is the Notto Prince. I am on a quest to find the Winged Unicorn," he said. "And once I do, it'll be all mine!"

The prince reminded Chelsea of another annoying boy.

The Notto Prince flew away with his jet pack. Chelsea knew she had to find the Winged Unicorn before he did!

"My spun sugar will help get you to your next destination," Barbie said to Chelsea, "if you believe in magic!"

Chelsea and Honey magically returned to their flying boat. It flew
them to the Wispy Forest, which was a land made of hair—and hares!
A hare named Locksley and a horse named Delia led Chelsea
and Honey to Shampoo Falls to meet the Princess Tribe. Surely they
would know about the Winged Unicorn.

When they arrived, Chelsea met the Forest Princess named Barbie. Barbie noticed Delia, and the princess's hair transformed into flower-tipped antlers.

"It's how I felt just now when I saw you coming out of the forest," Barbie explained. "Our hairstyles express our emotions."

Then Barbie felt silly, and her hair became the shape of an ice cream cone!

Another princess felt creative, and her hair looked like a musical note.

It seemed to be so much fun that Chelsea tried it, too!

Suddenly, an angry creature called a Mople interrupted their fun. He reminded Chelsea of the tangles she sometimes got in her hair.

"I'm mad hair!" he declared. "I don't want to calm down because then I might not be mad anymore. It's better to be mad than . . ." He paused and sighed. "Too late. Now I'm sad."

"I was sad, too. I thought I wouldn't be able to ride in the bike race with my friends," Chelsea said. "That's why I decided to find the Winged Unicorn. If I ride the Winged Unicorn, I'll be filled with magic. Then I'll be able to do anything I set my mind to."

The Notto Prince appeared and demanded that Barbie tell him where to find the Winged Unicorn. Barbie wanted to help Chelsea, but she knew the Notto Prince wouldn't leave until he had the information.

"The Winged Unicorn lives in another world not far from here," Barbie said, "but you have to find the sparkle dust to get close to it."

"I'm going to capture that unicorn and keep it all to myself!" the Notto Prince declared as he flew away. Chelsea knew that she needed to find that unicorn before the Notto Prince did! Her new friends rushed to help by getting her a bubble ride back to her boat.

Soon Chelsea and Honey arrived at Sparkle Mountain, where they found Barbie, the Apprentice Glitter Queen.

Everyone in the kingdom used their imaginations to create magic. When they worked really hard to imagine something, it happened!

Barbie was still working on her magic skills, but she loved to practice. She used her magic to create a gemstone necklace for Chelsea and a gem-studded collar for Honey!

Later, Chelsea met the castle cat, Melky.

"What a pretty necklace," Melky said, eyeing Chelsea's sparkling jewelry. "Does it contain sparkle dust?"

"Yes," said Barbie. It was exactly what Chelsea needed to find the Winged Unicorn! They disappeared in a poof of magic, leaving Melky behind.

Barbie, Chelsea, and Honey followed a trail of magical dust
left by the Winged Unicorn. Soon the trail led to a tiny hole in a
wall. It seemed they would have to end their quest, but Chelsea
had an idea!

"The sparkle dust!" she exclaimed. The magic worked, and
they all became small enough to fit through the hole.

As Chelsea and Barbie continued to trace the unicorn's trail, Melky and the Notto Prince appeared. Melky was working for the Notto Prince, who commanded Melky to pounce on the shrunken girls.

Luckily, Barbie used her imagination to make them invisible. They escaped just in time!

The Notto Prince discovered that Chelsea had dropped her gemstone necklace. With the sparkle dust inside it, he could do anything!

Meanwhile, Barbie, Chelsea, and Honey arrived at a reflecting pool. Barbie's friends Amethyst and Cobalt came up with a plan.

"You can use the reflecting pool to find the Winged Unicorn," Cobalt said.

Barbie used her magic. An image appeared in the water: the Winged Unicorn was in Rainbow Cove!

Chelsea didn't know how to get to Rainbow Cove without her gemstone necklace.

"You have inner strength," Barbie reminded her as she helped Chelsea and Honey on their way. "You just have to focus and believe!"

So Chelsea did exactly that.

It worked! With the magic of believing, Chelsea and Honey made it to Rainbow Cove and met Barbie, the Rainbow Princess. Here the princesses could swim in the ocean as mermaids and then transform into humans on land.

They saw the Notto Prince, but he was up to no good! He had caught the Winged Unicorn in a raindrop cage but had somehow locked himself in the cage as well.

Barbie assured Chelsea they could save the unicorn if they all worked together.

The princesses joined their color powers to form a beam of light. With Chelsea's and Barbie's help, they pointed the beam at the lock, which broke open. The Winged Unicorn was free!

Chelsea leaped onto the Winged Unicorn's back.
Together, they flew safely away from the Notto Prince.
    Suddenly, Chelsea realized she had achieved her goal!
"I'm riding the Winged Unicorn!" she cheered.
    Honey barked happily as Chelsea and the Winged
Unicorn sailed across the sky.
    Chelsea felt as if she were magical!

When Chelsea awoke from her dream, she was amazed by all the things she had seen and people she had met. Now she knew what to do for Fun Days!

Later that day, she arrived at the starting line of the bike race—with her training wheels.

"I haven't learned how to ride a bike without my training wheels," Chelsea confessed to her friends. "I was afraid to tell you."

"I just took my training wheels off a few months ago," Zoie said.

"And I can't ride very fast," Jace added.

Chelsea grinned. Her friends didn't care one bit about her training wheels!

Moments later, the race started. Chelsea rode as fast as she could.

Chelsea astonished everyone by crossing the finish line first.
"You did it!" said Barbie.
Chelsea smiled. Riding her bike had felt like magic!
And maybe it was!